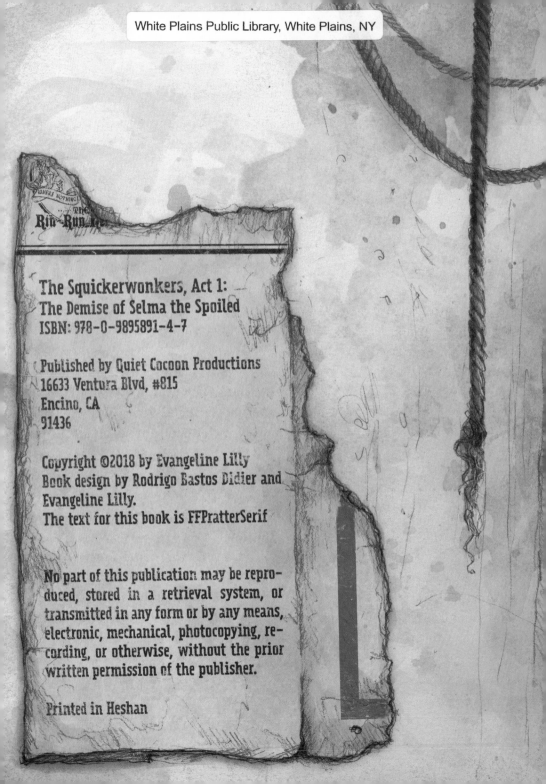

The Squickerwonkers, Act 1:
The Demise of Selma the Spoiled

ISBN: 978-0-9895891-4-7

Published by Quiet Cocoon Productions
16633 Ventura Blvd, #815
Encino, CA
91436

Printed in Heshan

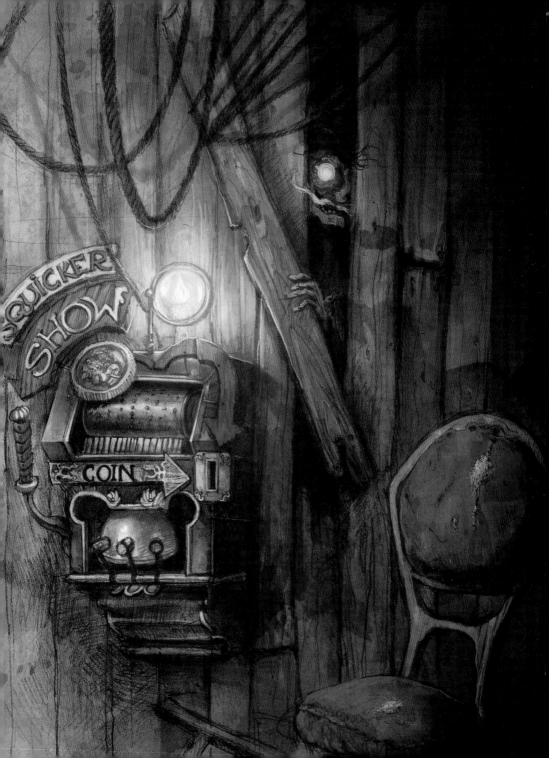

THE SQUICKERWONKERS
— now numbered ten; —

Selma's vice had gotten her foiled.
She had come to their hands
by her many demands
so they called the girl "Selma the Spoiled".

The Squickerwonkers

The Demise of Selma the Spoiled

EVANGELINE LILLY

Illustrated by

RODRIGO BASTOS DIDIER

NEW RIN-RU

THE • SQUICKER WONKER FAMILY VISIT RIN-RUN

PAPA THE PROUD

MAMA THE MEAN

ANDY THE ARROGANT

LORNA THE LAZY

MEGHAN THE

ROYALS IN TOWN

AN THE GUILTY · GREER THE GREEDY · GILLIS THE GLUTTONOUS · SPARKY THE SPECTACLE · SELMA THE SPOILED

"Give me a treat!
I want that dress!
I insist that you come out to play!"

It seemed nothing had changed,
for the girl was deranged
in her need to have things her own way.

"A much bigger toy! A jester for me!
I want my own traveling show!"

What Selma would choose
no one dared to refuse.
The answer could never be *no*.

When daily the Squickers paraded through town,
Selma came with a skip and smile.
It gave her great pleasure
to seek out some treasure
and add it to her growing pile.

She'd find sweets, and meats and treats galore,
all manner of laces and wigs.
She'd find bugs and mugs,
jugs, rugs, and pugs,
microscopes, rackets and figs!

Something exotic, something quite plain,
as long as to her it was new;
a washboard basin,
a gap-toothed mason,
the whole Rin-Run Jamboree crew!

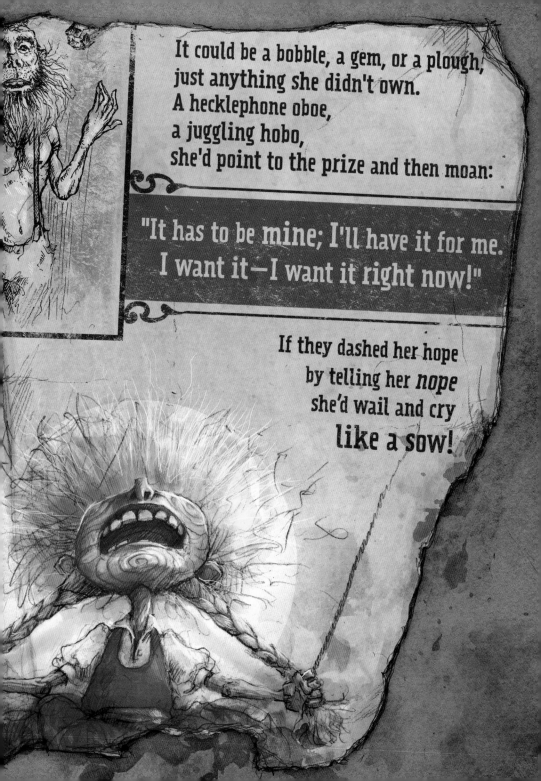

It could be a bobble, a gem, or a plough,
just anything she didn't own.
A hecklephone oboe,
a juggling hobo,
she'd point to the prize and then moan:

"It has to be mine; I'll have it for me.
I want it—I want it right now!"

If they dashed her hope
by telling her nope
she'd wail and cry
like a sow!

So *yes* was the answer the Squickers would give
to each of her crazy demands.
Then one fateful day,
to the Squickers' dismay,

a strange vendor arrived in their lands.

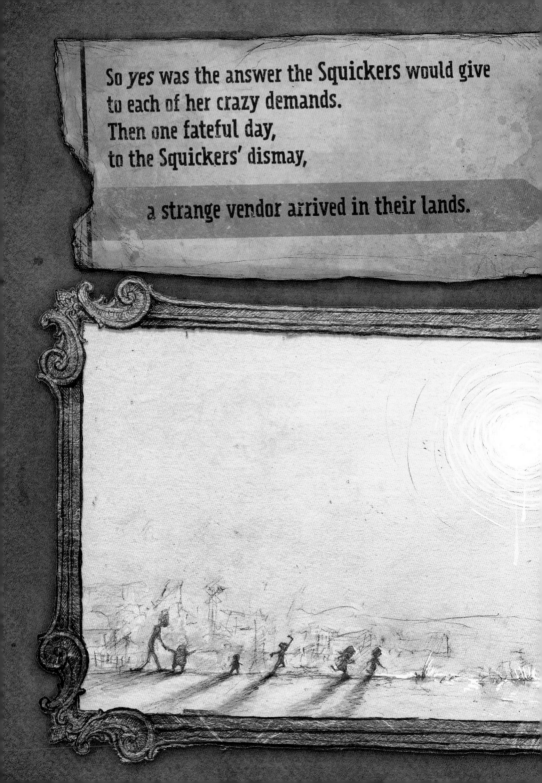

Pulling a barrow and singing a song,
this enchanting man called ahead,

❧

"Sweet children, come near,
the Jingle Man's here
and I've come with a marvelous spread!"

❧

"My wagon is brimming,
it's utterly swimming,
come see what this piper has got."

"I've got springs, and rings and mechanical things;
I've got bangles, and tinctures and dollies.
I've got snakes, and rakes,
and cinnamon cakes;
I've got gum-gums, and licorice and lollies."

What would you like? What is your dre___
Look at this sparkly hatt___
___ put the th___

But Selma just yawned with her nose in the air;
     she had all that regular stuff.
  Then, shaking his head,
                  the Jingle Man said,
    "I can see that this sale will be tough."

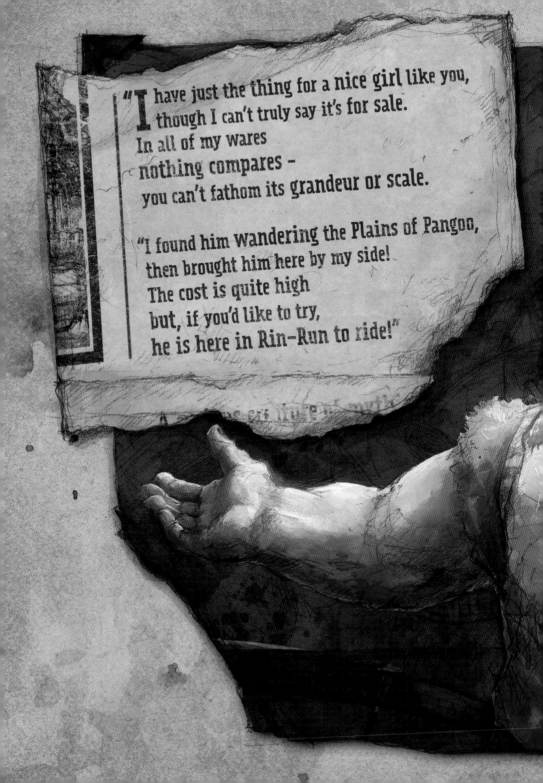

"I have just the thing for a nice girl like you,
though I can't truly say it's for sale.
In all of my wares
nothing compares –
you can't fathom its grandeur or scale.

"I found him wandering the Plains of Pangoo,
then brought him here by my side!
The cost is quite high
but, if you'd like to try,
he is here in Rin-Run to ride!"

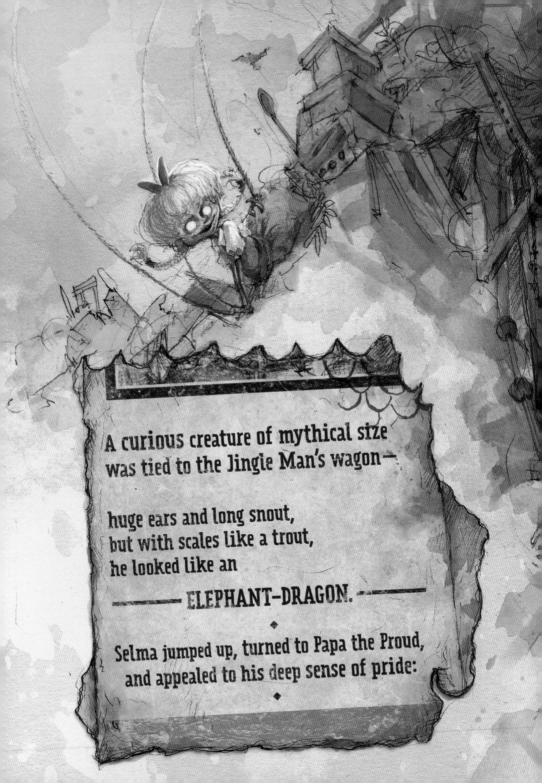

A curious creature of mythical size
was tied to the Jingle Man's wagon—

huge ears and long snout,
but with scales like a trout,
he looked like an

—— ELEPHANT-DRAGON. ——

◆

Selma jumped up, turned to Papa the Proud,
and appealed to his deep sense of pride:

◆

"As the
Lord of the Land,

make a gesture so grand
that your status will not be denied.

"A ride?
    A ride?"
that Jingle Man says,
    but he thinks like
a poor simple vendor.
    Oh, no, that won't do,
I expect more from you.
    Buy the beast!
Let's show Rin-Run your Splendor."

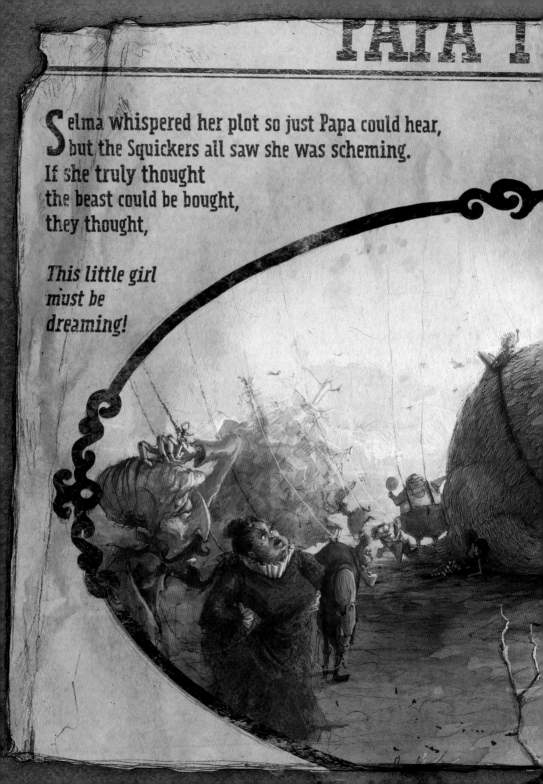

Selma whispered her plot so just Papa could hear,
but the Squickers all saw she was scheming.
If she truly thought
the beast could be bought,
they thought,

*This little girl
must be
dreaming!*

PROUD

"OF COURSE I'LL BUY YOU THE BEAST FROM PANGOO,"
Papa said with a grand show of stature.

And to say the least,
why he'd want such a beast,
for the Squickers,
was a real
head-scratcher.

"I think he's a blast," Sparky piped up to say.
"Have you ever seen such a big trunk?
Now calm your fears, Andy,
        I think he's just dandy.
Don't worry, you'll still be our our hunk."

Then scratching away on her little notepad,
Meghan drew her own plans for the beast:

Wearing a crown,
she would make it bow down
before cooking it up for a feast!

"Has anyone thought of the care it will need?"
Lorna moaned to her dear Aunty Greer.
"That beast will need tending,
its seat will need mending,
and there's no way that I'll volunteer."

But Greer the Greedy
was much too distracted
to pay her young niece
any mind.

much too distracted to pay
her young niece any mind

Her hair was all puffed
with Jingle Man's stuff;

SHE WAS ROBBING
THE POOR FELLOW BLIND!!

"Greer, my dear!"
exclaimed Gilligan the Guilty.

"You're taking this man's
livelihood!

"Oh, sir, please
don't blame her.
It's my job to tame her.
It's *me* who is not very good."

Watching the scene, big 'ol Mama the Mean stepped in to calm down her troupe.

"Let's not get hysteric,
this problem's generic.
We're used to strange things in our group.

"Yes, dearest Selma,
you may have your big beast,"

Mama sneered and patted her head.

BATHTUB MAN

g and brilliant news.
, our very own Bath-
Brooke, has not only
n his doorstep every
the past thirty years,
has been panning our
ery single day of those
...unfortunately, to no
is luck changed this
steadily under the un-
Run sun. Gideon spot-
light and a stroke of
onday, August 5 th of
s year, 1901! A whole
bble of gold rolled
pan and made him
n in heart, if not in
is side of Pangea.
Bathtub Man

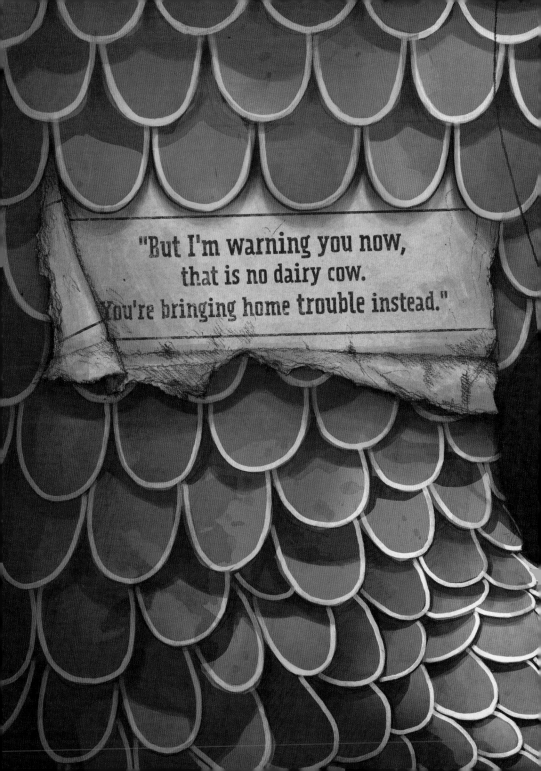

"But I'm warning you now,
that is no dairy cow.
You're bringing home trouble instead."

Papa gave Jingle Man a huge pot of gold
and he happily trotted away.
Selma looking so pure,
and *almost* demure,
announced,

"THIS IS MY HAPPIEST DAY!"

She then tied the beast to their wagon and rode,
parading her prize through Rin-Run.
Mama wore a strange smile
and then, after awhile,
warned,

"Beasts weren't created for fun."

"I'll do as I please;
I'm a big girl, you know!"
Selma yelled as they stopped at their door.

Then she up
and jumped out, with a whoop and a shout:
"And you're not my boss, you old boar!"

She squealed with glee and removed the big chains,
fed the beast with a savory treat,

• • •

then she dressed him all up
as a poodle-type pup
with a bonnet and lace on his feet.

Well...

It didn't take long
for the beast to get bored.
He decided to go for a roam.
He was much too distracted,
and **wildly attracted**

by the wonders of their
mighty home.

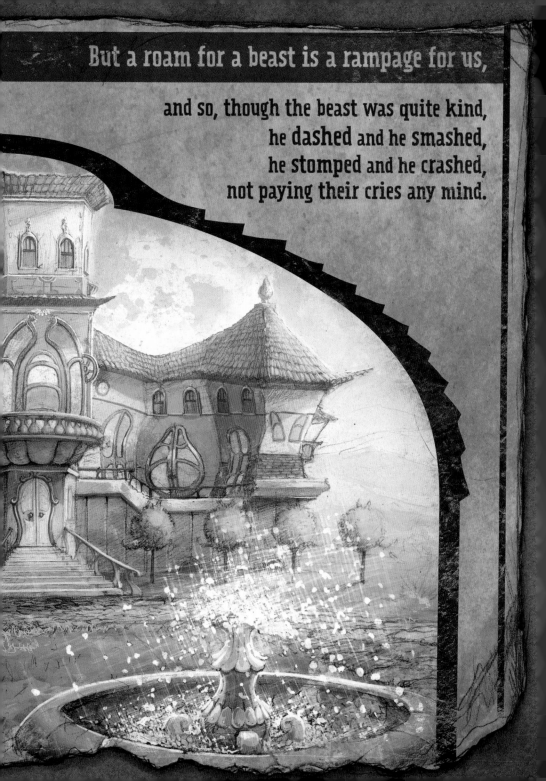

But a roam for a beast is a rampage for us,

and so, though the beast was quite kind,
he dashed and he smashed,
he stomped and he crashed,
not paying their cries any mind.

And cry Selma did, as I'm sure you could guess;
she'd never had such a big fit.
But despite all her ranting, her puffing and panting,
her pet simply just wouldn't sit.

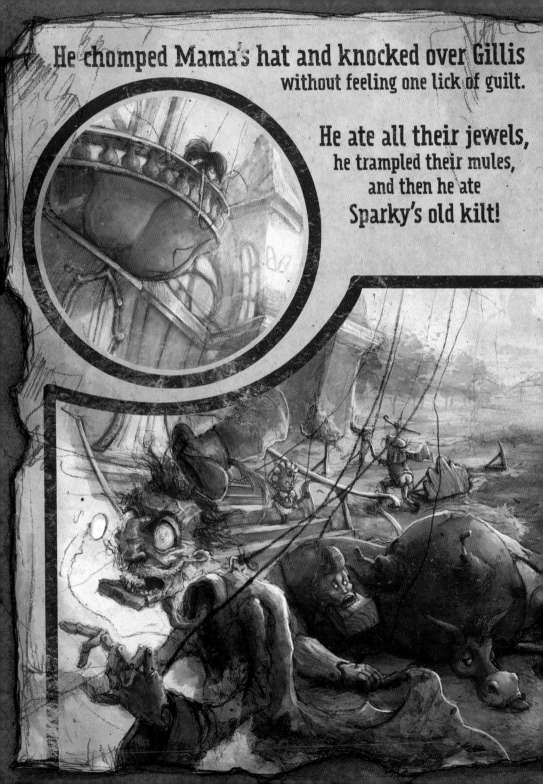

He ate all the bushes, the trees and the grass, but his hunger just grew and grew.

So, while Selma was pouting, and whining, and shouting,

The Beast from Pangoo ate her, too.

The End

MISSING

SELMA THE SPOILED
of the Rin-Run Royals

Who might be next to see their demise??
Will Andy, or Meghan or Greer?
Though Selma is gone
our tale carries on,
but where will it go from here...?

If spotted, please don't react. Walk slowly. Calmly tell one of your
COUNCIL OF RIN-RUN MEMBERS
DON'T MAKE A SCENE

EVANGELINE LILLY is a passion-
ate reader and writer who made her
publishing debut in 2014 when she
first introduced The Squickerwonkers
to the world. Though better known
for her portrayal of iconic characters
in film and television (LOST, The Hurt
Locker, Real Steel, The Hobbit, Antman
And The Wasp...), the Canadian actress
spends all of her down time creating
worlds of her own.

"Acting is my day job. Books are my life."

RODRIGO BASTOS DIDIER is an
artist from Recife, Brazil, who has
been bringing his imagination to life
through any artistic medium possible
since childhood. In his professional
career, Rodrigo has covered the gamut
- once a professor of art, he has also
created album covers for rock bands,
illustrated for magazines and worked
as a sculptor and painter of collectible
statues.

ANDY THE ARROGANT

PAPA THE PROUD

GILLIS THE GLUTTONOUS

LORNA THE LAZY

SELMA THE SPOILED